Grace,

The young lady that did this book is the daughter of Dr. Garcy corr, whom I worked for, for 17 Years. I remember when she was born. She is very talented.

I hope you enjoy reading this to Eden.

Written by Emma Maiorana   Illustrated by Gayle Cobb

Love to be Loved

Illustrated by Gayle Cobb

Printed in the United States of America
Published by Braughler Books LLC., Springboro, Ohio

First printing, 2021

ISBN: 978-1-955791-21-2 soft cover
ISBN: 978-1-955791-22-9 hard cover

Library of Congress Control Number: 2021921921

Ordering information: Special discounts are available on quantity purchases by bookstores, corporations, associations, and others. For details, contact the publisher at:

sales@braughlerbooks.com
or at 937-58-BOOKS

For questions or comments about this book, please write to:
info@braughlerbooks.com

Braughler™
Books
braughlerbooks.com

To my family,
and everyone involved in making this dream come true.

One fine morning,
as they woke with a yawn,

brothers, Bruce and Obie,
thought of the places they've gone.

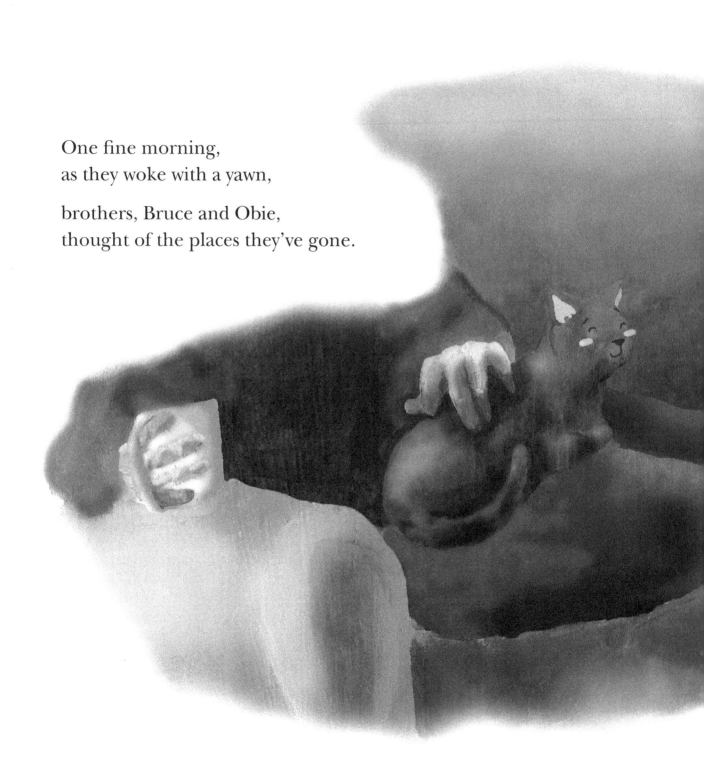

"Where haven't we been yet to explore and discover?"
"How about the rescue ranch?" Obie asked his brother.

"That sounds like fun!
  I wonder who we'll meet."

And with much excitement,
  they set out for an adventure quite neat.

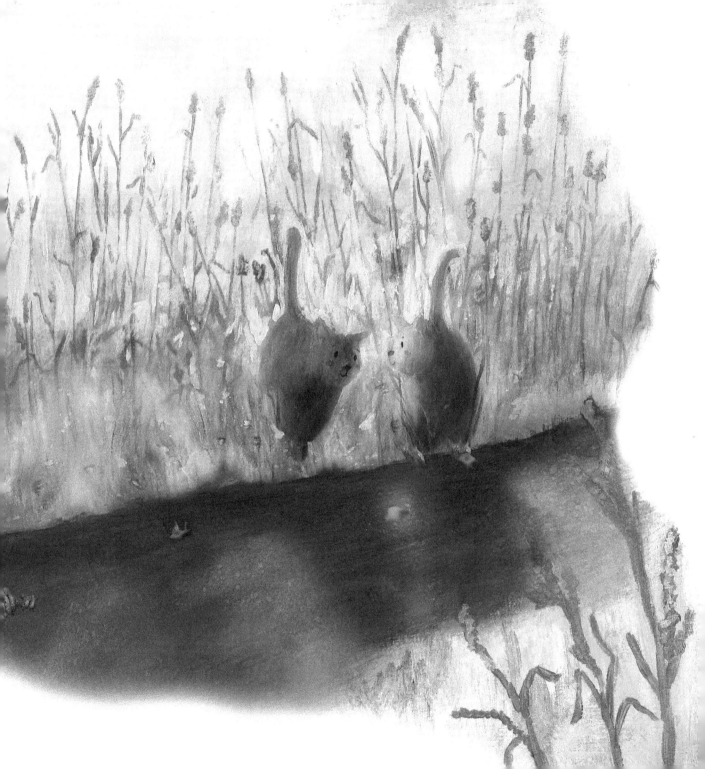

Past the thick of the woods and down a winding path, the brothers saw a red barn. The rescue ranch at last!

Up on a hill, in the shade of old oak trees,
were black and white spots enjoying the breeze.

"Hello, there!" the brothers said together.
"How *doooo youuuu doooo*?" replied a special heifer.

"We're great!" they purred.
"We've never met a cow before, you're the first one.
  We were wondering—what do you like to do for fun?"

"Well, I don't only moo, jump over the moon, and swat flies,
I like to prance, dance, and watch the sunrise!

"I may not be a pet like you and live in a house and such,
  but I love to be loved, just as much."

Down a grassy trail that led to a field,
was a big round belly enjoying a meal.

"Sa-a-a-lutations!" said the goat, shaking his billy goat chin.
"What do you like to do for fun?" asked Bruce with a grin.

"Not only do I *baa-aa-aa-aaaa*,
chew, and eat,

I like to frolic, climb, and … eat.
I really do love to eat.

"And I may not be a pet like you or sleep in a bed and such,
but I love to be loved, just as much."

Across the field, as the journey pursued,
were silky smooth feathers together in a brood.

"Greetings!" Bruce announced with delight.
"Hi, there!" clucked the chicken with a smile so bright.
"What do you like to do for fun?" Obie asked in the warm sunlight.

"Well, not only do I *bok-bok-bok*, cross roads, and lay eggs,
I like to roam free, take baths, and stretch my legs!"

"I may not be a pet like you or play with toys and such,
 but I love to be loved, just as much."

In a lush pasture stood a very large crowd,
of what looked, to the cats, like fluffy white clouds.

"Good afternoon," Bruce and Obie kindly said.
"Hello, hello," replied the sheep with a nod of her head.
"What do *ewes* like to do for fun?" the cats asked instead.

"We're not only counted when tired
and provide people with wool,

we like to play games and
make new friends!
We're really quite social.

"We may not be a pet like you and get belly rubs and such,
but we love to be loved, just as much."

Next to the barn was a group of muddy pink snoots—
and when he looked down, Obie saw his new muddy boots.

"Howdy!" the furry felines yelled.
To which the pig oinked, "Howdy to you as well!"
"What do you like to do for fun?" the cats asked, hoping he'd tell.

"Well, I don't only forage, roll in mud,
then sleep when I'm done,
I like music, massages, and laying in the sun.

I may not be a pet like you or nap on a couch and such,
but I love to be loved, just as much."

"We may look different and play different games,
but wanting to be cared for is what makes us the same.

We may not come from a house, but from a farm or ranch,
and we make just as good friends if you give us a chance.

"Whether a cow or pig or goat and such,
we loved to be loved, just as much."

About the Author

Writer, poet, and animal lover, Emma Maiorana was inspired to pen *Love to be Loved* by the inherent bond between children and all living creatures big and small, house-trained and farm-raised alike, and the undeniable proof that all animals truly love to be loved. Emma was born in Florida, grew up in Virginia, and made a life for herself in Pittsburgh, Pennsylvania, where she currently resides.

About the Illustrator

Gayle Cobb is a freelance Illustrator based in Cincinnati, Ohio. Having attained a Bachelor's of Science in Illustration from Indiana Wesleyan University, Gayle has since illustrated numerous books for both traditional and self-publishers alike.

Learn more about the artist at: *www.gcillustration.com*

CPSIA information can be obtained
at www.ICGtesting.com
Printed in the USA
BVHW021530050422
633383BV00002B/12

9 781955 791229